The Magic School Bus®
TO THE RESCUE »»»»»»»»»»»
BLIZZARD

SCHOLASTIC INC.

New York   Toronto   London   Auckland   Sydney
Mexico City   New Delhi   Hong Kong   Buenos Aires

The author would like to acknowledge Jonathan D. W. Kahl,
Professor of Atmospheric Sciences at the University of Wisconsin,
Milwaukee, for his advice in preparing this manuscript.
Also, special thanks to Charley Shimanski, Education Director
of the Mountain Rescue Association for offering a real-life
perspective of snow rescue and the generosity of volunteerism.

Written by Judith Stamper.

Illustrations by Ted Enik.

Based on *The Magic School Bus* books
written by Joanna Cole and illustrated by Bruce Degen.

ISBN 0-439-42939-0

12 11 10 9 8 7 6 5   4/0 5/0 6/0

Designed by Peter Koblish

Printed in the U.S.A.   40

First printing, November 2002

INTRODUCTION

Hi, my name is Carlos. I am one of the lucky students in Ms. Frizzle's class.

Maybe you've heard of Ms. Frizzle. (Sometimes we just call her the Friz.) She is a terrific teacher — especially if you like excitement and surprises. Sometimes things can get really strange in her science class. The Friz *loves* science, and she will do *anything* to teach us about it.

We go on lots of field

trips in the Magic School Bus. Believe me, it's not called *magic* for nothing. Once we get on board, anything can happen — and it does!

We can usually tell when the Friz is planning a new science unit — we just look at what she is wearing. One day, Ms. Frizzle came to class wearing a dress covered with skiers. That was our first clue. When the Friz put on a matching parka and ski boots, we knew it was field trip time. Soon we were off on a wild winter adventure!

CHAPTER 1

I rushed into Ms. Frizzle's classroom, excited to show everyone my new snowboard. It's an awesome board that I got for my birthday. But just as I stepped through the door, I slipped and ended up sliding across the floor — on the seat of my pants!

"Whoa!" I yelled. "What's going on? I'm not even on my board — and I'm bailing!"

Bailing, in case you didn't know, means crashing or falling down in snowboarding talk. And I bailed right into Ms. Frizzle's desk!

"Carlos, you slid right through my snowman!" Arnold yelled.

"What snowman?" I asked, picking my-

1

self up off the floor. I looked down and saw some icy water under my feet.

"My science experiment," Arnold moaned. "It was already melting, but now it's just a pile of slush."

"I'm sorry, Arnold," I said. "But that snowman didn't have a chance in this weather."

We were studying winter weather in science class, but the weather outside wasn't cooperating. It was December, and the temperature still hadn't gotten close to freezing. I was itching to use my new snowboard, but there wasn't a flake of snow around!

"It's 55 degrees Fahrenheit out today," Dorothy Ann said with a groan, checking the thermometer outside our window.

"It isn't like winter at all," Tim said.

Just then, Ms. Frizzle swept into the room like a one-woman blizzard. She was wearing a dress covered with a snow-sport design. "Good morning, class!" she called out. "How do you like my new dress?"

"It's pretty cool, Ms. Frizzle," I said.

"Carlos!" everybody yelled. But that didn't stop me. "Cool and sporty," I added.

Everyone groaned at my joke.

"That dress might be the most snow we see all winter," Dorothy Ann said. (We usually just call her D.A.) "I don't think global warming is fair to kids. We haven't had a chance to play in the snow."

"It's hard learning about winter weather," Tim said, "when it's warm outside."

Global Warming: A "HOT" Topic
by Dorothy Ann

Planet Earth is heating up. Ever since the 1980s, the earth's average temperature has gone up. Why? Many scientists believe it's because more and more gases like carbon dioxide are filling the atmosphere. The gases trap the heat from the sun inside the atmosphere — and that warms up our world!

"I want to see snow, sleet, freezing rain — all that winter wet stuff," Keesha said. "I'm doing my project on winter precipitation."

Wet Winter Weather
by Keesha

When it's winter, get ready for some wild wet weather!

Snow Flurries: light snow that falls for a short time with little or no accumulation BR!

Sleet: raindrops that freeze into pellets of ice before they reach the ground BRR!

Snow Squalls: brief, intense snow accompanied by high winds with major accumulation BRRR!

Blizzard: Heavy snow and blowing winds more than 35 miles per hour (56 kmph) resulting in near-zero visibility BRRRR!

"I want to go snowboarding," I added. "I took lessons last winter, and my instructor said I had some slick moves on the slopes." I couldn't help but sneak a peek at the full-page photo in my extreme snow sports magazine.

"All I want is to make a real snowman that doesn't melt," Arnold said. "My project is on what kind of snow packs best. So far, I've had to make my own snow in an ice crusher!"

"We've hit a dry spell," Ms. Frizzle said, "and there can't be any snow if there isn't any moisture in the air. We need some of our good friend water vapor."

From the Desk of Ms. Frizzle

Water: It's Not Always Wet!

Water can exist in three forms:
1. Solid (like snow and ice)
2. Liquid (like rain and lakes)
3. Gas (water vapor)

Water changes between these states all the time. It's obvious when water falls from the sky as rain and snow. But an equal amount of water is always floating back up into the sky. You just can't see the water going up because it's in the form of an invisible gas called water vapor. Water vapor forms clouds, then changes into rain or snow before falling down to Earth.

"Well, kids," Ms. Frizzle said, "if the snow doesn't come to us, maybe we can go to the snow."

"Are you talking about a field trip?" Arnold asked in a worried voice.

"I just got this postcard from my friend Brian Russell," Ms. Frizzle said. "He lives in the Rocky Mountains in Colorado."

Ms. Frizzle read the postcard aloud.

Dear Valerie,
The snow has been falling for several weeks out here in the Rockies. It's perfect for skiing and snowboarding. You and your class are welcome to visit. It's a great place to learn about winter weather.
Brian

We all crowded around the Friz to look at the postcard. On the front was a picture of two snowboarders. They were zigzagging down a snow-covered mountain.

"Wow, would I love to hit those slopes!" I said. "You see that guy out in front? He's doing an alley-oop. I learned that trick last winter! I hope I remember how to do it." The guys on the postcard looked pretty good.

"It must be awesome to live in the mountains," I said. "I bet he goes skiing and snowboarding all the time."

"He does — and not just for fun," Ms. Frizzle said. "He also leads a Mountain Rescue Team."

"What's that?" asked Ralphie.

"When there's a blizzard, skiers can get lost in the snow and it's his job to find them," Ms. Frizzle told us. "Winter weather is full of all kinds of danger."

"Danger?" Arnold asked nervously.

"Brian said that the blizzards in the Rockies can be so intense that you can't even see an inch in front of you," Ms. Frizzle explained. "That's why they need a Mountain Rescue Team to go out and rescue people lost in a storm."

From the Desk of Ms. Frizzle

The Snowcapped Rockies

The Rocky Mountains are the largest mountain chain in North America. They stretch more than 3,000 miles (4,800 km) across the continent, from northern Alaska to northern New Mexico.

The peaks of the mountains are so high that they are cold enough to be covered with snow year-round. The snowy winters in the Rockies make them a great place for winter sports — and blizzards!

"I wouldn't get lost in a blizzard," I said. "I'd just jump on my snowboard and whiz right through it." I couldn't figure out how

people could be afraid of the snow. Snow is all about fun!

"Maybe we don't have to see winter weather in person," Arnold said. "These paper snowflakes are okay with me."

"I think it's too late now," Keesha whispered. "Look at Ms. Frizzle!"

Ms. Frizzle had gone to the supply closet. She was busy putting on a mountain-covered parka. I could see the class lizard, Liz, scurrying around getting the Friz's ski boots from the back.

"Who's ready for some real winter weather?" Ms. Frizzle asked.

Everybody but Arnold screamed, "Me!"

"Come on, Arnold," the Friz said. "Don't let a little snow give you cold feet. You can make a snowman."

"Well, okay," Arnold said. "As long as we don't get stuck in a blizzard."

I guess Ms. Frizzle didn't hear Arnold say that, because she was already at her computer, typing an e-mail to Brian.

"I'm telling Brian that we're on our

way," the Friz said as she clicked the SEND button. Then she headed out the door for the Magic School Bus. We all ran after her and climbed on board.

"Wow, that snow looked superdeep in the Rockies," I said to Tim.

All I could think about was swooshing down those snow-covered slopes. I had no idea that we might get in too deep!

CHAPTER 2

"Hey, Carlos, sit with me," Tim called from across the aisle. "I want to see your snowboard."

I grabbed the seat next to Tim in the Magic School Bus. We were just starting to check out my board when Ms. Frizzle made an announcement.

"Fasten your seat belts, kids," she said. "And stow your backpacks and gear under the seats."

Tim and I looked at my snowboard. It was too big to fit.

"What about Carlos's board?" Tim called out.

"Don't worry, Carlos," the Friz said. "You won't be bored for long!"

Everyone groaned except me. I was the only one who thought Ms. Frizzle's joke was hilarious!

"Can I stow my board in the back, Ms. Frizzle?" I asked.

"Just hurry up, Carlos," the Friz said. "We're ready to roll!"

She was right about that! As soon as I got back to my seat, the Magic School Bus started up with a roar. It zipped down the road, and before you could say wahoo, the bus turned into a jet.

Soon, the ground was whizzing by in a blur. Then the Magic School Jet zoomed up into the sky. WHOOSH!

"Colorado, here we come!" Dorothy Ann yelled.

As the jet headed west toward the Rockies, we all settled in for the trip.

In front of me, Phoebe was busy wrapping up Liz in her striped winter scarf.

"Don't worry, Liz," Phoebe said. "You can ride in my parka hood if it gets really cold."

I pulled out my snowboarding magazine and looked at it with Tim. We read an article about my favorite professional snowboarder.

"Ms. Frizzle," Arnold called out. "Do you think we'll really see snow? Maybe global warming has gotten to the Rockies."

"Just look out the window, Arnold," the Friz said.

Every head in the jet leaned toward the windows to get a look. Outside, the sky was filled with white stuff.

"Excellent!" I yelled. "We're in snow country!"

"I didn't think we'd see that much snow," Ralphie said.

Just then, the jet's loudspeaker crackled on.

"This is the National Weather Service," a deep voice said. "A winter storm watch is in effect. Severe winter conditions are likely to begin soon."

Mountains: A Hotbed for Snow
by Ralphie

To have a lot of snow you need three things:

1. It has to be cold. Mountaintops are cold because they're high above ground level. It gets colder the higher it is.

2. The air has to have lots of water vapor. The Rocky Mountains receive winds from the Pacific Ocean and the Gulf of Mexico that are full of water vapor.

3. The air must rise. As air rises, it cools, and the water vapor condenses to form clouds and snow. When wind blows into a mountain, the air rises because it can't just blow through the mountain.

"Ms. Frizzle," Wanda said, "that guy gave me goose bumps! What's a winter storm watch?"

"I know," Phoebe said. "That's what I'm doing my report on."

Winter Weather Watch
by Phoebe

Winter Storm Watch: Severe weather such as heavy snow or ice is possible in the next few days.

Winter Storm Warning: Severe weather conditions have begun or will begin very soon.

Blizzard Warning: Heavy snow and strong winds will produce blowing snow, near-zero visibility, deep drifts, and life-threatening windchill.

"Well, at least it's only a winter storm watch," Arnold said weakly.

A second later, the loudspeaker came on again.

"This is the National Weather Service," the voice said. "A winter storm warning is now in effect. All aircraft should exercise necessary caution."

I looked out the window. The snow was getting thicker and thicker the farther west we flew. I had a few goose bumps now, too!

"Well, at least it's only a winter storm warning," Keesha said.

Suddenly, there was a loud beep over the loudspeaker. We all jumped.

"This is the National Weather Service," the deep voice said. "A blizzard warning has just been put into effect. All aircraft should land as soon as possible."

"Ms. Frizzle," Dorothy Ann called out. "What are we going to do?"

"Fasten your seat belts tighter, kids," the Friz said. "We're going in for a landing!"

My ears began to pop as we lost altitude. I wasn't sure how the Friz could see where we were going. The snow was white, and the sky was, too.

We hung on to our seats and watched the Friz at the controls. She checked the radar screen and brought the jet in for a landing in a snow-covered valley.

Finally, we hit the ground. I expected to land with a big bump, but the Friz kept it nice and smooth. Then I felt the brakes pull the plane to a stop.

"We're here, kids!" the Friz sang out.

"Where's here?" Arnold asked nervously.

"Pile out of the plane," the Friz said, "and you'll see."

We grabbed our gear and made for the exit. When we stepped out of the plane, did we ever get a surprise!

The Rocky Mountains rose up before us in high peaks. They were enormous — and absolutely white with snow. We stood and stared at them. Then I looked around and realized that we were all snowcapped, too! The flakes were big and fluffy and were piling up fast on our heads and shoulders.

Suddenly, we heard a horn honk. We turned around to see Ms. Frizzle behind the wheel of the Magic School Bus again. But it looked different — its wings were gone. Now it had a big snowplow attached to the front.

"All aboard," the Friz yelled. "We're still several miles away from Brian's lodge. And we've got to climb a mountain to get there!"

We all scrambled on board the Magic School Snowplow. Ahead of us, we could see the narrow road that snaked up the side of the mountain. On one side of the road a rocky cliff rose straight up; on the other side was a steep fall. The little guardrail didn't look like it would do much to stop us if we wandered off the road!

From the Desk of Ms. Frizzle

Giving Snow the Shove

Snowplows are the workhorses of winter weather. The blade on the front of most snowplows can be adjusted to different positions.

The "V" position is the best position for making a first pass through heavy snow. The blade comes to a point in the middle. This point cuts through the snow, which is pushed away from the road by both sides of the angled blade.

"Ms. Frizzle?" Arnold asked nervously. "Isn't this the kind of weather you're not supposed to drive in? What if we get stuck in the snow?"

"You're absolutely right, Arnold," the Friz said cheerfully. "It would be very unsafe to drive an ordinary car in a blizzard like this. But this is a snowplow — and a magic one at that!"

The Friz lowered the plow and headed up the mountain. The snowplow bulldozed right through the piled-up snow.

"Look out, Rocky Mountains, here we come!" I yelled. I just hoped the Friz could find the road under all that snow. The last thing I wanted was to get too close to the edge!

The snow was getting thicker and thicker as we climbed higher and higher up the mountain. When we looked out the windows and down the side of the mountain, we could hardly see a thing. Every once in a while we'd notice the lights from a cabin, but the roads were empty.

"Wow," I said. "I wonder how high up we are now."

"I don't want to know!" Phoebe said with a shiver.

Phoebe was right to be nervous, I guess. The roads hadn't even been salted, like they are at home after a big snow.

Salt, Sand, and Snow
                                        by Phoebe

Why does putting sand or salt on a snowy road help people drive?
• Sand makes a rough surface that car tires can grip.
• Salt makes water melt at temperatures it normally wouldn't – so the snow on the road melts and goes away!

Ms. Frizzle just kept her eyes on the road. The headlights of the snowplow cut through the snow ahead of us.

"Ms. Frizzle, I see something," I yelled. "Look, up ahead."

Farther up the mountain, the road led right to a cozy cabin built out of huge wooden logs.

"That's it," the Friz said. "Let's see if anyone's home." She pulled the snowplow into the parking lot in front of the lodge.

We all piled out of the snowplow and headed for the door of the lodge. The wind was blowing harder and the snow was falling even faster.

"I think the blizzard warning is turning into a real blizzard!" Keesha said.

What Is a Blizzard, Anyway?
by Keesha

What's the difference between a blizzard and an ordinary snowstorm? A blizzard is a winter storm with:
- lots of fine, dry, powdery snow
- winds of over 33.5 miles per hour (53.9 kmph)
- very cold temperatures
- so much snow in the air that you can only see a few yards

Ms. Frizzle knocked and then pushed open the door of the lodge. We all followed her. It was dark inside.

While Ms. Frizzle tried to find the light switch, we took off our coats and piled them in the corner. But before she could turn on the lights, we heard a growling noise from the other side of the room.

"What's that?" Arnold said, his voice quavering.

In the dark, we could just make out the shape of a large, furry animal lumbering toward us.

"Augh!" screamed Arnold. "It's attacking me!"

CHAPTER 3

Ms. Frizzle laughed. "Don't worry, class," she said, flipping on the light.

We all looked over at Arnold. A big Saint Bernard was licking his hand. I mean a *big* Saint Bernard. The dog wagged his tail at Arnold, who smiled sheepishly.

Ms. Frizzle reached down and patted the dog.

"Class, meet Snowball, another good friend of Brian's," the Friz explained. She looked around the lodge at the big fireplace and empty chairs. "Hey, Snowball, where's everyone else? They didn't leave you alone, did they?"

"They're probably all taking advantage of the fresh powder on the slopes. I think we should be out there, too," I told the Friz. "I don't want to sit around here and wait for them. Let's go!"

But before Ms. Frizzle could say anything, a telephone on the wall rang. She picked it up.

"I'm sorry, Brian doesn't seem to be here right now," she said. "Is this an emergency?"

I ran over to the Friz. "Who is it?" I asked.

"It's the local sheriff," she said. "Some people are stranded in their car. They called 911 on their cell phone, and the sheriff thought Brian might be able to help them."

The Friz turned her attention back to the telephone. "Yes, of course, I'll tell him as soon as he returns," she said. "You say they're on the road that winds through the forest from Point Baldy to the Powder Trail? . . . Yes, I've got that . . . Okay, I'll tell him."

Just then, we heard the door to the lodge open. A young man came bursting into the room, along with a gust of snow. I noticed his snowsuit right away. It was just like one I saw in my snowboarding magazine.

"Who are you?" he asked in surprise. "Did you get caught in the blizzard?"

"I'm Valerie Frizzle," Ms. Frizzle said, reaching out to shake his hand. "And this is my class. I e-mailed Brian that we were coming."

"I'm Luke, Brian's cousin. I remember Brian talking about you. Don't you drive some kind of special school bus?"

"The Magic School Bus," I said. "I'm Carlos, by the way. Do you snowboard?"

"I love to snowboard. That's why I'm staying with Brian," Luke said. "Want to go out when the blizzard stops?"

"That would be awesome," I answered.

"Speaking of the blizzard," Ms. Frizzle interrupted. "A call just came in. Some people are trapped in a car. Is there some way we can let Brian know?"

"I can try to reach him," Luke said. "He's out with the Mountain Rescue Team right now. He asked me to come back here to hold down the fort. I guess it's a good thing I did."

"Ms. Frizzle, can we go out and try to find the stranded car?" I asked. "We didn't come to Colorado to sit inside a lodge and play tiddledywinks." I hoped Ms. Frizzle would agree.

"You're right, Carlos," Ms. Frizzle said. "We can do something to help."

"Tiddledywinks sounds like fun to me," Arnold said.

"Luke, tell Brian that we're out searching for the people who called in," Ms. Frizzle said. "Class, follow me."

"Are you sure you should be driving?" Luke said. "It's pretty nasty out there."

"Oh, a little snow won't stop the Magic School Bus," the Friz said. She pulled her parka hood tighter around her face and headed out the door. I was right behind her. I couldn't wait to see some snow action!

"Yikes!" I said the minute I stepped outside the lodge. "Ms. Frizzle, where are you? I can't see a thing!" The white snow was swirling all around us. I felt like I was in the mid-

die of one of those snow globes you shake —
only the globe was twice as full of snow!

"It's a whiteout, Carlos," I heard the Friz
yell. "Isn't it exciting?"

Winter Weather Q & A
by Carlos

What is a whiteout?

In the middle of a bad blizzard, snow is blown in all directions by strong winds. The air is filled with blinding, blowing snow. That's a whiteout!

Why are whiteouts so dangerous?
It's easy to get lost in a whiteout. People have even lost their way only a few feet from their front doors!

Whiteouts are particularly dangerous for pilots, who may have difficulty determining which way is up.

"You kids hang on to one another!" the Friz advised.

"But Ms. Frizzle," D.A. yelled, "how can we drive the bus in this weather? Isn't it dangerous?"

"It's too snowy for the Magic School Bus," the Friz called out. "And it's far too snowy for the Magic School Jet. But Mother Nature has a way of getting around in the snow. Just a minute!"

I guessed we'd have to wait. We couldn't see well enough to do anything else.

Ouch! I felt someone step on my foot, but I couldn't see anyone in front of me. I reached out and grabbed someone's hand. "It's me, Carlos," I said.

"It's Ralphie."

Slowly, we all found one another. Then we heard a loud whistle, followed by a powerful swooshing sound in the air above us. The snow cleared for a moment. And something big came in for a landing right in front of us.

"It's an eagle!" Dorothy Ann shrieked.

Ms. Frizzle was standing next to a huge golden eagle whose eyes looked suspiciously like the Magic School Bus's headlights. The Friz had on aviator's goggles and looked like Amelia Earhart — except for the hair, of course.

"This is Goldy," Ms. Frizzle said, patting the eagle's head. "Climb on board and find yourself a comfortable feather."

"Come on," I yelled, beating everyone else onto the eagle's back. I snuggled in just behind the Friz. The rest of the kids tucked themselves in behind me.

From the Desk of Ms. Frizzle

Big Birds

Colorado is home to both golden eagles and bald eagles. The golden eagle lives in rugged cliffs and canyons. It is dark brown with a wash of golden feathers on its head and nape. The bald eagle has a white head and tail.

Eagles are powerful fliers, strong enough to wing through the fierce winds and heavy snow of a blizzard. A golden eagle can reach flying speeds of an estimated 150–200 miles per hour (240–320 kmph)!

"Put on your goggles, kids," Ms. Frizzle said. "We're taking off!"

The eagle lifted its wings and began to soar toward the sheer drop at the end of the parking lot. Just before we got to the edge, Goldy caught the wind under its wings — and soon we were soaring high above the mountains.

"Where are we going, Ms. Frizzle?" Phoebe yelled out from Goldy's tail feathers.

"We're going to try to find the stranded couple. It will take us a while to get to that part of the forest, but keep your eyes peeled!" Ms. Frizzle explained.

Down below us, we could see the white snow from the blizzard. But now we were above the storm, and the air felt warmer!

"What's going on, Ms. Frizzle?" Tim said. "My goggles are fogging up!"

"Goldy just flew into a warm, moist air mass," the Friz explained. "It came from the warmer climates down south. But at the same time, a freezing air mass from the Arctic north swept into the United States from Canada.

Kids, this is where a winter storm begins. You're about to see how snowflakes form!"

From the Desk of Ms. Frizzle

The recipe for a winter storm calls for one warm air mass and one cold air mass. The lighter, warm air will rise up over the heavier, cold air. And as the wet, warm air cools down, the clouds start to shrink. The smaller clouds can't hold their moisture anymore, and the moisture falls out and freezes into snowflakes.

WARM, WET AIR

COOL, DRY AIR

"Snowflakes!" Dorothy Ann said. "I'm doing my project on that."

"Then let's go take a close-up look," the Friz said. "Hold on tight, everybody!"

A Snowflake Is Born
by Dorothy Ann

1. A tiny drop of water falls out of a cloud. The cloud is high in the sky, where the air is very cold.
2. The droplet grows and freezes into an ice crystal.
3. At about 5° Fahrenheit (−15° C), the crystal grows six branches with arms.
4. The crystal grows bigger and heavier and begins to drop.
5. As the crystal drops, supercooled water vapor hits the crystal and freezes on it, changing its shape.
6. As the crystal falls, it may melt onto other crystals and form a bigger snowflake.

"Whoaa!" Arnold screamed as Goldy took a nosedive into where the warm air and the cold air met. Soon we were surrounded by beautiful snowflakes falling out of the clouds around us.

Dorothy Ann whipped out her camera. "Cool," she said. "I can get some close-ups for my snowflake project."

"Hey, D.A.," Tim asked, "is it true that every snowflake is different?"

"According to my research," Dorothy Ann answered, "most snowflakes have a basic six-arm structure. Sometimes two melt together to make a 12-arm formation. But each one is flaky in its own way."

I was enjoying the ride, but I was also very cold. And that made me think about the people who were stuck in the forest.

"Ms. Frizzle," I said. "Are we getting close to that stranded car? Those people must be pretty cold by now."

"We're almost there, Carlos," the Friz said. "That peak just ahead is Point Baldy."

Then she added, "Hang on to your stomachs, everybody. This might be a wild ride!"

I grabbed hold of one of Goldy's feathers as the eagle swooped down in the sky. As we dove out of the clouds, we had a bird's-eye view of the top of the Rockies. Goldy made a circle around one of the peaks and then swooped down into a valley. It looked so peaceful, soaring up high and seeing everything covered with snow. Normally, all I would have been thinking about was how great it would be to tackle the hills on my snowboard. *As soon as we find that car,* I thought, *I'm all over those slopes.*

Just then, Phoebe screamed. I looked up to see that we were headed straight for a tree.

"We're going to crash!" Tim yelled.

CHAPTER 4

"Don't worry, kids," Ms. Frizzle said. "Goldy has got everything under control." We landed with a soft rustle on a branch at the top of a tall fir tree.

We caught our breaths and watched the snow fall around us. The wind had quieted down, and the whiteout had cleared up.

Ms. Frizzle opened up her backpack and handed me pairs of binoculars to pass back to everyone.

"Look carefully, kids," the Friz told us. "Those stranded people should be somewhere very near here."

Goldy raised its wings, and we lifted up

off the top of the fir tree. Then our eagle-bus soared over the green fir trees of the mountain forest.

For a few minutes, we anxiously scanned the snow in silence. There seemed to be a hush over the entire world . . . until Wanda said excitedly, "Look! Over there!"

We all looked down to the ground where Wanda was pointing. "Sorry — it's just a dog."

"Actually, I think that's a coyote," Tim said. "You can tell by its tracks."

The coyote was picking its way through the snow, leaving tracks behind it.

"And there's a deer," Ralphie added. "No, two deer!"

"Wow," Dorothy Ann said, peering through her binoculars. "You can see animal tracks everywhere in the snow."

As we watched, the animal tracks began to disappear under the newly fallen snow. It made me think about how much snow had fallen since we first got the emergency call at the lodge.

Be a Track Detective

by Tim

See if you can match the tracks below with the animals that made them. Here is the list of animals to choose from:

- deer
- rabbit
- coyote
- raccoon

A. B. C. D.

Answers: A. deer, B. rabbit, C. raccoon, D. coyote

43

I looked at Ms. Frizzle, who was intently scanning the road below with her binoculars. I had a feeling that she was thinking about the stranded people, too.

"Keep following this road, Goldy," Ms. Friz said to our eagle. "They've got to be around here somewhere."

"Look! Up ahead, Ms. Frizzle," I said excitedly. "I think that's the rescue team. And they're helping people out of a car. Maybe they're the people who called!"

"You're right, Carlos," the Friz said. "It must be the rescue team. I can see their special orange jackets from here. And I think I recognize my friend Brian!"

The Friz brought Goldy down for a landing in a clearing not far from the rescue workers.

"Say good-bye to Goldy for now," the Friz said. "We're coming to the rescue in the Magic School Snowmobile!"

There was a sudden flurry of feathers everywhere, and before we knew it we were sitting in the seats of a big snowmobile!

Ms. Frizzle revved up the motor, and we flew across the snow toward the rescue workers.

"Valerie!" a surprised-looking man said as Ms. Frizzle came to a stop near the rescue team. "How did you get here? There's been a terrible whiteout!"

"Hello, Brian," the Friz said calmly. Then she patted the top of our bright yellow snowmobile. "We came in on the Magic School Snowmobile."

"Well, I'm glad you arrived safely," Brian said. "You flew in during the middle of one of the worst blizzards I've ever seen. And blizzards can be bad news for a lot of people!"

"That's why we're here," the Friz said. "When we got to the lodge, I answered a call from the sheriff about some people who had been stranded in the snow — and we came out to find them."

"I know," Brian explained. "Luke got hold of us on the radio. He told us the location the people gave you, so we knew right where to find them."

From Brian's Rescue Patrol Handbook

Bad News Blizzards

Big blizzards cause big problems. Here are just a few of the dangers:
- Fallen power lines cut off the supply of electricity.
- Frozen pipes cut off water and fuel sources.
- Poor visibility closes airports.
- Heavy snow can cause roofs to collapse.
- People caught in blizzards can suffer frostbite and hypothermia.
- Heavy flooding can result when all the snow melts.

And there's all that snow to shovel away!

Just then, two rescue workers carried a man from the stranded car right past us on a stretcher.

"Thanks for coming to help," the man said through chattering teeth.

"Will he be okay?" I asked Brian.

"As soon as we get him back to the lodge, he'll be fine," Brian said. "We checked both of them out for frostbite and hypothermia. It was a close call, but we got here just in time."

"Can you check me out for frostbite?" I joked. "I think that the blizzard nibbled at my nose."

"If you had frostbite, your nose would know it!" Brian replied. The way he said it, I knew frostbite was no laughing matter. But he still took the time to check out my nose.

From Brian's Rescue Patrol Handbook

A Funny Name for a Serious Danger

Frostbite is a great concern for people who are caught out in the cold. In extreme conditions, ice crystals can form in the skin or beneath the skin — which means part of the skin is actually freezing. In severe cases, the skin tissue dies. This is called gangrene, and it can cause people to lose fingers and toes.

As Brian looked at my nose, I got kind of nervous. He explained the first signs of frostbite to the class. "When it's really cold, your body tries to keep you warm and protect itself. Your blood vessels constrict, or become smaller, to try to keep the warmth in your body. The bad part of this is that it means there is less blood making it to your extremities, like your fingers, toes, nose, and ears, so they get pretty cold. That's why it's important to protect your extremities by wearing warm boots, gloves, and a ski mask."

Brian carefully looked at my nose and ears from all angles, which made me feel bad since I had just been joking about having frostbite. "The early signs are when a patch of skin looks pale," Brian continued. "That's because there isn't any blood getting to it. The best treatment for frostbite is to soak the skin in warm, not hot, water. And you shouldn't rub the skin, because that could cause the blood vessels to break."

Brian said that he thought I looked okay, but we should all get back to the lodge. "The snow may have slowed down, but the wind is still mighty fierce. I bet Luke has some hot chocolate waiting on the stove for us. It's just what we need."

Brian was right. The wind was strong, and that made it feel even colder. The windchill factor is one reason blizzards are so dangerous.

From Brian's Rescue Patrol Handbook

The Windchill — A Freezing Formula

Wind makes the temperature on a cold day feel even colder! This chart shows what wind can do:

Wind Speed When the wind blows . . .	Temperature and the thermometer reads . . .	Windchill Factor the temperature really feels like . . .
10 mph (16 kmph)	10° F (-12° C)	-4° F (-16° C)
20 mph (32 kmph)	10° F (-12° C)	-9° F (-23° C)
30 mph (48 kmph)	10° F (-12° C)	-12° F (-24° C)

We already knew that frostbite could injure our extremities, but then Brian told us about hypothermia — which is what happens when your whole body gets too cold. The facts were bone-chilling, and I'm not kidding.

Snow safety is serious stuff.

Hypothermia: Don't Mess with the Cold!

Hypothermia occurs when your entire body becomes dangerously cold all the way through. It is the number one cause of death for people taking part in outdoor activities.

Cold weather is most dangerous when:
1) you get wet
2) you are exhausted
3) it is very windy

It does not have to be below freezing for hypothermia to strike — in fact, most cases occur when the temperature is between 30 and 50 degrees Fahrenheit (-1 and 10°C)!

I offered to help Brian load up the shovels and other rescue equipment the team had used to pull the people out of their car.

Then he asked if I wanted to ride back to the lodge with the rest of the rescue workers.

Did I ever! On the way back, I listened to the workers talk about the other people who had been trapped by the blizzard that day. The rescuers were so brave and friendly, I even forgot about snowboarding for a while!

When we all got back to the lodge, Arnold stared up at the icicles hanging from the eaves of the roof. "Hey, that's what I feel

like," he said with a sniffle, pointing to the biggest one. "An icicle with a drippy nose!"

That night we all slept in sleeping bags on the floor of the lodge, right in front of the warm fireplace. But I wasn't thinking about warm things . . . I was dreaming about the snowboarding I would be doing the next day!

CHAPTER 5

The sun woke us up the next morning, shining through the window like a bright spotlight.

"I slept like a bear!" I said with a big yawn.

Arnold sat up straight. "Did someone say bear?" he asked, looking around. "I just dreamed a bear licked me."

Tim started laughing. "That was Snowball," he said.

"I guess you were *barely* asleep, Arnold," I said. Tim groaned and pulled his sleeping bag over his head.

Just then, Ms. Frizzle knocked at the door, shouting, "Last one up is an Abominable Snowman! Hurry and eat breakfast," she said. "It's time to get some hands-on experience with your snow projects!"

We jumped out of our sleeping bags, ate breakfast, and pulled on our snow gear.

When we opened the door of the lodge, did we ever get a surprise! The snow on the ground came up to our waists! Someone had dug a path out from the door. It looked like a tunnel through a mountain of snow!

Ms. Frizzle scooped up a handful of snow. "If anyone wants to throw snowballs, do it now while the snow is still fresh and fluffy! If it melts and gets icy later, snowballs would be too dangerous."

"This snow is perfect," said Arnold. "It doesn't get any stickier than this!"

"Yippee!" Tim yelled. He took a flying leap into a snowdrift. I followed right behind him.

Phoebe and Wanda laid down in the

snow and made snow angels with their arms and legs. Ralphie and Keesha each started to build a snow fort, while Arnold began to roll the bottom ball of a snowman.

When Snow Is Sticky
by Arnold

Sometimes when you scoop up a handful of snow, it forms a snowball right away. Other times, no matter how much you squeeze, you still have a handful of loose powder.

The temperature and liquid content of the snow determines how well snow sticks together. Cold, dry snow makes a fluffy powder that doesn't stick together much. But if the snow is a little wetter and the weather gets a little warmer, the snow will be sticky — perfect for making snowballs, snow forts, and snowpeople.

I stood up, my whole body covered with fluffy white snow. The snow around us was such a bright white that it almost hurt my eyes.

"What makes snow so white, anyway?" I asked, examining a handful of white crystals.

Tim shrugged. "What makes anything white?"

Snow White
by Dorothy Ann

Snowflakes have many complex surfaces that reflect light. When the white light of the sun hits snow, almost all of the light reflects off of the snow. So snow looks white.

Most surfaces absorb some sunlight, which gives them their color. For instance, black things absorb all light. Blue surfaces reflect back blue light and absorb other colors. But white surfaces reflect all light.

"I know. I just did a report on that," Dorothy Ann said. "White light is a mixture of every color of light. The crystals in snowflakes reflect all the colors that make up sunlight, so they appear bright white."

All of a sudden, we heard Wanda give a yell.

Ralphie grinned and dove behind his fort to make another snowball. Wanda scooped up some snow and ran after him.

Just outside the lodge, the Friz was hiding behind a snow-fort wall with Keesha and Phoebe beside her. Keesha and Phoebe were busy making snowballs that they were feeding to Wanda. Wanda was taking aim at Tim and Ralphie, who were both crouched behind his fort. As everyone else threw snowballs, Arnold was trying to finish his snowman while dodging the flying white missiles.

"That's no fair!" I shouted. "It's three against two. Tim and Ralphie, I'm here to save the day!"

I ran behind the boys' fort and started to

make snowballs. We were just beginning to win when Brian came out of the lodge.

Brian was carrying a measuring stick. We stopped throwing to watch him.

"Twenty-five inches," he said after he poked the stick into the snow. "That's not a record for these parts. But it's a lot of white stuff."

"Wow," Ralphie said. "Colorado must get the most snow in the country!"

"Nope," Brian said. "That happens in New York State. It gets a lot of extra snow because it is so close to the Great Lakes. The extra moisture in the air means more snow."

Lakes and Snow
by Ralphie

Mountains aren't the only places that get lots of snow. Water evaporates from very big lakes and forms clouds that dump tons of snow nearby. Cities right next to the Great Lakes, like Buffalo and Rochester, New York, can get almost 100 inches (254 cm) of snow each year!

The rest of the kids went back to playing in the snow. But I went over to talk to Brian.

"Uh, Mr. Russell," I said, wanting to be polite.

"Forget about the Mr. Russell stuff. Just call me Brian," Brian said.

"Okay, Brian," I said, "do you think I could hit the slopes pretty soon? I really want to try out my new snowboard. And maybe you can tell me some more about being on a Mountain Rescue Team."

"As a matter of fact, I'm going to check out the condition of the ski trails right now," Brian said. "Want to come along?"

"That would be excellent," I said. "Let me grab my snowboard."

"Sure, but wait a minute," Brian said. "You should ask Valerie, I mean Ms. Frizzle, first."

I promised Ms. Frizzle I would do anything for her if she would let me go — even clean out Liz's habitat every day.

The Friz came through and said yes.

YES!

Soon I was zooming along a perfect trail on my snowboard behind Brian. He flipped around and did a fakie, and I followed right behind him.

If you haven't been snowboarding, a fakie means riding backward. I had practiced that a lot last winter.

"You're good, Carlos," Brian yelled. Then he turned to face forward.

On our way down the hill, Brian stopped every so often to check on the condition of the snow.

"What are you looking for?" I asked.

"After a big snow like this," he explained, "we have to see how the snow has packed on top of itself. Sometimes there is a weaker layer of snow underneath a stronger layer. And that can make the snow on top start sliding down the slope."

I looked around at the tons of snow covering the mountains. For the first time, it looked kind of scary.

"Are you talking about an avalanche?" I asked.

"Right," Brian said. "But this snow is in perfect condition. It's the same density all the way down. There shouldn't be any problems with an avalanche here."

"That's good," I said nervously. "'Cause there's a lot of white stuff around!"

From Brian's Rescue Patrol Handbook

Strong Snow and Weak Snow

A "weak" layer of snow is one that can't hold the layer above it in place. This can cause an avalanche if the top layer starts sliding. Weak layers can occur when:
- a dry, powdery layer of snow is underneath a layer of wet, heavy snow
- an old layer of snow buckles under the weight of a new layer
- rocks or trees cause snow to pile up in a way that is unstable
- strong winds blow snow into drifts and slabs

We hiked up to a slope with a lot of direct sunlight on it, and Brian took two shovels out of his backpack. He handed one to me.

"What's this for?" I asked.

"The best way to check the snow conditions is to dig a snow pit," he said. "That way you can see exactly how the snow looks at different depths."

As we dug, he explained that some of the slopes in the area had gotten a lot of sun in the past week. Sunlight can melt the top layer of snow, which freezes again to form ice. This can create a "lubricating layer" — a hard, slippery layer that can make the snow on top of it start sliding. He said we were checking to make sure the new snow that had fallen wasn't sitting on top of a lubricating layer.

When we had dug down a couple of feet, Brian showed me a place where the snow got harder. "That was the top layer before yesterday's blizzard," he said. We kept digging until we had a hole deep enough to stand in.

"Well," Brian said. "It looks safe here. But I'm still concerned about what could happen in places where the wind piled the new snow up higher." We climbed out of the snow pit and put the shovels into his backpack.

"Let's head back to the lodge now," Brian said, hopping back on his snowboard. "I want to get reports from the people who are out checking other parts of the mountain. Everything always looks so beautiful covered in snow, but it can be a white nightmare! No smart skier or snowboarder should go out into the backcountry without carefully assessing the hazards first."

From Brian's Rescue Patrol Handbook

Triggering an Avalanche

Most avalanches that occur naturally take place in remote areas where no one is around. Avalanches that involve people are usually triggered by the victims themselves.

People can trigger an avalanche just by skiing over a layer of snow that is unstable. Anything that causes vibrations — like a snowmobile — can also dislodge snow and start an avalanche.

Places that are at greatest risk for triggering avalanches include:

- the very top and bottom of a slope
- places where a lot of new snow has fallen
- places where wind has piled snow into drifts

We were definitely in the backcountry — there were no ski lifts or roads and not many people. It made for exciting skiing, but it was also dangerous.

Fortunately, the snow was perfect. We shot down the mountain, weaving back and forth through the fresh-fallen powder. I had a little trouble keeping up with Brian, but he slowed down for me every once in a while. By the time we got back to the lodge, my legs were sore, but my mind was soaring! There was a lot more to backcountry snowboarding than I had thought.

When we got back to the lodge, Brian went inside to check his e-mail. I stayed outside and told Ms. Frizzle all about what Brian had taught me.

"That sounds like a good topic for a report, Carlos," she said.

A minute later, Brian came running back out of the lodge. "Valerie, where are the rest of the kids?" he asked in a worried voice.

What Beats an Avalanche Rescue?
Preventing Avalanches!
by Carlos

The National Ski Patrol rescues skiers in trouble. But its members would much rather prevent an avalanche accident from happening in the first place. To prevent avalanches, they clear out snow before it gets to dangerous levels so the slopes are more stable. They do this by:

- skiing along the top of slopes to send a "sluff" of loose snow sliding downhill
- dropping small explosives on slopes

The Ski Patrol works mostly in resort areas. The backcountry is just too large to clear off every slope.

CHAPTER 6

I looked around. Where were Tim, Wanda, and Dorothy Ann?

"They went for a snowboarding lesson," Ms. Frizzle said. "Luke offered to take them."

"Did Luke say where they were going?" Brian asked.

"Yeah, he said to tell you they were going to the Little Wolf Trail," Ralphie piped up.

"Brian, what's wrong?" I asked.

"I just got an e-mail from the Avalanche Forecast Center," Brian said grimly. "Snow conditions are deteriorating in that area — fast. They've issued an avalanche warning.

Luke and the kids are right in the middle of the danger zone."

"Come on, class," the Friz said, rushing over to the Magic School Bus. "We've got to find Tim, D.A., Wanda, and Luke."

"But you can't get to them in that bus," Brian said.

"Climb aboard," Ms. Frizzle said. "We'll get to them."

Seconds later, we were lifting off the ground in the Magic School Helicopter. Our friends were somewhere out there. And we had to find them — before it was too late!

The sound of the helicopter's rotor blade pounded in our ears as we flew over the snow-covered mountains. My heart was beating almost as loud. Suddenly, the snow below us looked dangerous again. I was worried about Luke, Tim, D.A., and Wanda. What if they were caught in the path of an avalanche!

"Ms. Frizzle," Phoebe warned, "there's another helicopter up here! We don't want to crash!"

Brian and Ms. Frizzle caught sight of the copter Phoebe was talking about. It was painted orange and had a special symbol on the side.

"That copter belongs to the avalanche controllers, Phoebe," Brian explained. "They help stop big avalanches by starting little ones."

"How do they do that?" I asked.

"Just watch," Brian said. "And listen."

We saw something drop from the orange helicopter. A few seconds later, there was a burst of light followed by a loud boom. A puff of snow rose up from the mountainside. Then we heard a rumble as the snow began to move.

Right in front of our eyes, we saw the side of the mountain begin to slide down. As snow from the top came down, it pulled more snow with it. The snow fell in a heap at the bottom of the mountainside.

"Wow! What happened?" said Phoebe.

"They dropped an explosive charge to make the snow start sliding," said Brian. "The National Ski Patrol does a lot of preventive work like this in resort areas," Brian said.

"But out here in the backcountry, the Department of Transportation does it. They can't cover the entire state, though. It's just too big. They only clear the snow from places where an avalanche could block a road. Everywhere else, the snow just piles up."

"We'd better find Luke, Tim, D.A., and Wanda fast!" I said to Ms. Frizzle.

"Head north," Brian told the Friz. "That's where the Little Wolf Trail is."

As Ms. Frizzle turned the copter north, Brian explained more to us about avalanches.

"There are two kinds of avalanches," Brian said. "A loose snow avalanche starts at a single place on top of a mountain. As it moves down the mountain, it gets bigger. Its path looks like an upside-down V."

"Is that the worst kind of avalanche?" I asked. It sounded pretty bad to me.

"No way," Brian answered. "The worst kind is the slab avalanche. It's more dangerous because it's big from the beginning. A slab is a big block of snow that breaks loose from the layer of snow beneath it. The slab slides

73

down the mountain with a huge amount of force and weight."

The Magic School Helicopter soared to the north. Somewhere down there, Luke, Tim, D.A., and Wanda were risking their lives — and they didn't even know it!

"Are there always avalanches after a heavy snow in the Rockies?" I asked with a shudder.

The Big Boom!
by Keesha

A large avalanche in the United States can dump as much as 300,000 cubic yards (230,000 m³) of snow down a mountainside. That's as much as 20 football fields filled 10 feet (3 m) deep with snow.

During a period of 50 years, more than 500 avalanche fatalities were reported in fifteen states.

"It all depends on the weather conditions. Colorado has the highest number of avalanche deaths in the United States," Brian said. "But we're working hard to keep those numbers down with our rescue teams by teaching people how to avoid avalanches."

"Why is today such a dangerous day for avalanches?" Ms. Frizzle asked as she piloted the copter between two mountain peaks.

"There can be a lot of reasons for avalanches," Brian explained. "Sometimes it can be because of too much snow falling on a mountain slope. Sometimes it can be because of a disturbance by a snowmobile or a skier. And sometimes it's because of a quick warm-up in the weather. Have you ever noticed how the snow sticks onto a car window after it snows? But the next day, after the sun has warmed up the snow, it suddenly slides off the window in a big chunk."

"Is that what's happening now?" I asked.

"Today the biggest problem is wind blowing all this new snow into drifts. Some of them are piled way too high," Brian said.

From Brian's Rescue Patrol Handbook

Diagram of an Avalanche

An avalanche is the natural effect of gravity on snow that lands on an incline. The three things that impact an avalanche are snowpack (layering of snow), terrain (incline of slope), and weather.

Starting zone: where the snow breaks loose
Track: the path the snow takes
Run-out zone: where the snow and debris come to rest

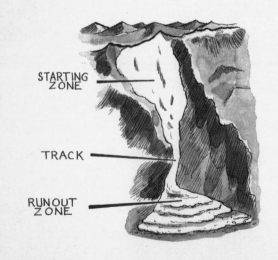

"That sounds pretty serious," Arnold said. "What would happen if the snowdrift started to slide?"

Brian pointed out the window. "Look down below us right now. You can see where an avalanche happened last month. There's the starting zone at top, the track down the mountain, and the run-out zone below. Even though it's been a month now, you can still tell how intense the fallout was."

I was staring down at the avalanche track when Ms. Frizzle suddenly let out a yell.

"There they are!" She pointed down the side of the mountain we had just flown over.

I looked down and saw four snowboarders on the fresh powder of the mountain. I could recognize Tim, D.A., and Wanda from their clothes. Wanda started slowly boarding across the slope by herself, while Luke and the others waited behind.

"How come Wanda's going all by herself?" I asked. "Why aren't they sticking together?"

"Luke knows the danger they're in,"

Brian said in a worried voice. "He's making them go one at a time so that if an avalanche occurs, only one will be affected, and the others can come to the rescue. Also, a bunch of people moving at once can actually start an avalanche. In fact, most avalanche victims trigger the avalanche themselves."

Ms. Frizzle flew the helicopter over Luke and the kids. I saw them look up when they heard the noise overhead. They saw the yellow color of the Magic School Helicopter and Luke started to wave like crazy. Then D.A. and Tim joined in. Wanda started walking back to the group.

"They see us!" I said. "They're waving for us to land."

"Not really," Brian replied. "Believe it or not, Carlos, waving your hands over your head is the signal for a helicopter NOT to land. It means it's not safe. And Luke is right. A helicopter landing could set off a tremor in the snow. You know what that could do."

I knew what it could do. It could set off

an avalanche. And Tim, Dorothy Ann, Wanda, and Luke would be at the bottom of it!

"So how do we help them if we can't land?" Keesha asked.

"We'll have to lower a rope ladder and do a midair rescue," Brian said. "Valerie, can you hover in the air above them?"

"Of course," Ms. Frizzle said with a determined look on her face. "The Magic School Helicopter can handle anything."

"This is going to be cool!" I said.

"It's going to take a lot of cool," Brian said solemnly. "Everybody is going to have to stay calm and help the kids and Luke into the copter without shaking up the snowdrifts."

Ms. Frizzle was as calm as ever at the helicopter controls. She piloted the helicopter over the kids and Luke, then hovered in the air like a big hummingbird.

Brian opened the hatch at the bottom of the copter and dropped down the rope ladder.

I watched the expressions on Tim's, Dorothy Ann's, and Wanda's faces turn from happy to worried. Luke said something to them, and they all unhooked themselves from their snowboards.

"Luke knows what we're doing and why," Brian explained. "He couldn't have known when he came out with the kids that the snow conditions would deteriorate so fast, but he knows why we're here with the copter. All the ski instructors on the mountain have been trained in avalanche safety."

Luke helped Tim up onto the rope ladder first. We watched as Tim struggled to climb up, step after step. Finally, Brian and I helped pull him to safety inside the copter.

"Tim!" I said. "Glad you made it!"

D.A. followed. She scrambled up the rope ladder like a pro, and we pulled her in.

Wanda was next. But she looked scared. I could see the tears glistening in her eyes. Luke lifted her up onto the ladder. She took a couple of steps, but when she tried to move up to the next rung she slipped.

Everybody sucked in their breath and then looked to the top of the mountain. A

crack had opened in the snow near the top of the slope.

"Luke," Brian yelled down, his eyes still on the top of the mountain. "Pick her up and carry her up the ladder. Now!"

Luke lifted Wanda up and draped her over his shoulder, then climbed up the ladder. When Luke was close enough, Brian reached down and grabbed hold of Wanda. She looked scared. But not as scared as the rest of us!

We could see the fracture growing bigger and bigger at the top of the mountain.

"It's coming down!" Tim yelled. "An avalanche!"

A moment later, Luke and Wanda were both safely inside the copter. The Friz zoomed straight up into the sky . . . without a second to spare!

There was a terrible rumbling noise above us. And then the snow came crashing down the mountain. It looked like it was moving in slow motion. But Brian knew better.

"Higher, Valerie," Brian was yelling. "Gain altitude!"

We just made it! Tons of snow came roaring down the mountain below us. We saw pine trees snap like toothpicks. The snow rushed like a white river into the valley beneath the mountain.

"Ms. Frizzle," Tim said weakly, "thanks for the ride!"

"It's good to have all of you on board," she said with a smile. "Let's get you back to the lodge."

"I'm glad you didn't have to find out firsthand how to survive an avalanche," Brian said. "But I'm going to go over it with all of you when we get back to the lodge."

As we soared back up over the mountains, I thought about everything I had learned about snow in just one day. And suddenly I knew that I had changed my mind about what I wanted to be when I grew up. I didn't want to be a professional snowboarder anymore. I wanted to be a mountain rescue worker!

From Brian's Rescue Patrol Handbook

How to Survive an Avalanche

1. Make sure you wear an avalanche beacon and have it turned on. If you get caught in an avalanche, a rescuer can home in on a signal even under feet of snow.

2. If you are caught in an avalanche, get rid of as much of your gear as possible to lighten your weight.

3. Use swimming motions to work your way up to the top of the snow.

4. Try to maintain an air pocket in front of your face, so you can breathe. Use your hands and arms to punch a hole in the snow in front of you.

5. Don't panic. Breathe steadily and conserve your energy until you are rescued.

CHAPTER 7

As we flew back to the lodge, our radio crackled on. "Brian, this is Gwen with the rescue patrol," a woman's voice said. "There's been an accident on Falcon Hill! Are you near there?"

"Yes! I'll be there in a couple minutes," Brian answered. He pointed toward a nearby peak, and Ms. Frizzle sent us zooming in that direction at top speed.

"One skier is fine, but his two friends got caught in an avalanche," Gwen said. "We'll meet you there as soon as we can."

"Got it. See you there," Brian said.

He set down the radio. "Okay, listen up,"

he said in a determined voice. "Every second counts, so do exactly what I say. We've got some people to rescue. Here's what we're going to do."

Brian turned to Ms. Frizzle. "What kind of rescue gear do you have in this helicopter?" he said.

Ms. Frizzle smiled and pointed toward the back. "The Magic School Helicopter should have everything you'll need."

"Good. Hand me that bag, please, Keesha," Brian said.

Keesha passed Brian a heavy bag. He opened it and started passing out equipment. "These are called beacons," he said. "They send out a radio signal that tells where you are."

He looked around seriously. "We're going into a dangerous situation, and my first responsibility is protecting you. Keep your beacon set on 'transmit' at all times, until I tell you otherwise." He made sure we knew how to switch them from 'transmit' to 'receive' before continuing.

From Brian's Rescue Patrol Handbook

A Beacon in the Snow

Beacons are the best way to find someone trapped by an avalanche. A beacon is a
radio-signal device that helps rescue workers find people buried in the snow, and it
works like a walkie-talkie. When skiing,
boarding, or hiking, you should set the beacon to "transmit" a signal. Rescue workers
also wear beacons, but they set their sig-
nals to "receive." Their beacons
will track the transmitted sig-
nals, so they can narrow their
search.

"These long metal poles are called
probes," Brian said, holding one up. "They're
used to search for people buried under the
snow. When using probes, it's important to
stand in a straight line, with no gaps."

The probes were too big to pass out inside the helicopter. They were 12 feet long and
a half-inch thick and were made of solid
metal. They looked heavy. "We've got some
shovels in here, too. Excellent," Brian said.

"Now when we land, the first thing we'll do is determine our escape route, in case there's another avalanche. You four will help Luke do a scuff search," he said, pointing to Ms. Frizzle, Tim, Arnold, and Keesha. "That means you'll kick through the snow, looking for clues like a hat or a ski pole that might tell you where the people are buried. Carlos, D.A., Ralphie, Wanda, and Phoebe, you'll help me do a beacon search. Then we'll get to work with probes and shovels wherever we find a clue."

From then on, everything happened incredibly fast. Ms. Frizzle set the helicopter down near a man in a blue-and-white ski jacket. Brian made us wait until the rotors stopped spinning, then he jumped out and we all followed. We could see where the track of the avalanche ended in a pile of debris. Brian showed us our escape route, then he spoke calmly to the man in the ski jacket, whose name was James. James was shaking, but he answered Brian's questions.

Brian asked James to use a ski pole to mark the spot where he had last seen his friends. Then he told Luke's search team to start at the bottom of the debris pile and work their way up to the pole.

"Okay! Everyone switch your beacons to receive — now!" Brian called. He stuck an earpiece into his ear and told me, D.A., Ralphie, Wanda, and Phoebe to do the same.

Everyone switched their beacons from transmit to receive. There was no sound from the beacons. We walked around the site for a minute or two in silence. Then Brian told everyone to switch back to transmit.

"What's wrong?" I asked. "Do you think their beacons are broken?"

"No," he said. "James said none of them were wearing beacons. But you should always check, just in case." He tossed me a shovel. "It's too bad. A beacon could have led us right to them."

"Hey, Brian!" Arnold yelled. "Look! A hat!"

"Don't move it," Brian called, running over. Phoebe and I raced after him.

Brian had Ms. Frizzle and Phoebe probe

and dig near the hat while Arnold kept searching. A moment later, Keesha found a ski pole. "Your turn, Carlos," Brian said, pointing to my shovel. He gave a shovel to James, too, and we both started to dig.

I couldn't believe how hard the snow was. I dug with all my strength. Suddenly my shovel hit something.

I scooped out some snow and saw a boot. "There's someone down here!" I yelled.

"Dig toward the head," Brian shouted. He joined me and James and began sending snow flying as fast as both of us put together. Within seconds we saw a red parka. We immediately started digging where it looked like the head would be. The snow moved beneath us, and an arm struggled out of the snow. Then a woman sat up, gasping and coughing.

James knelt beside her, brushing snow from her face. "Don't try to move her," Brian said quietly. "She could be hurt."

"Where's my husband?" she cried.

I heard another helicopter approaching. Brian looked up. "That's Gwen with the paramedics," he said. "They'll take care of you," he told the woman. "And don't worry. We're working to find your husband as fast as we can."

When the helicopter landed, a rescue team member followed a German shepherd as it dashed around with its nose to the snow. "The dog will find him if we don't," Brian said.

Search and Rescue Dogs
by Phoebe

SAR, or search and rescue, dogs are lifesavers after an avalanche. The dogs are trained to find "pools" of human scent, even if they are buried beneath feet of snow. The dogs work quickly and accurately, leading human rescuers to the buried victims.

Brian told two women in orange jackets to follow us with shovels, while two paramedics took care of the woman.

I was beginning to worry. We'd been searching about a half hour already. The man might not have much time left.

From Brian's Rescue Patrol Handbook

Every Second Counts

Snow rescue is a race against time. If recovered in 15 minutes, 90 percent of persons buried in avalanches survive. After 35 minutes, the survival rate falls to 30 percent.

Arnold and the others doing the scuff search had made it all the way up to the ski pole marker James had left, but they hadn't found any more clues. Brian called them over. "We're going to start a probe line now," he said.

Everyone lined up elbow to elbow in a perfectly straight line at the bottom of the search area.

"Probe!" Brian called. We all jammed our probes into the snow between our feet and pressed down as far as they would go.

"Step!" he yelled, and the whole line moved forward about a foot. Moving this way, we could cover a pretty big area, without leaving any big gaps.

I had worked up a sweat while I was digging, but now I was getting cold. We had to find the buried man, and soon. I hated to think what it would be like to be trapped under the snow.

A Lifeline to Survival
by Ralphie

An avalanche rescue crew often works in a line to find a buried avalanche victim. The searchers stand shoulder to shoulder and move down the slope. They have probes, or long poles, that they insert into the snow to try to find a victim.

"Hey! I think I hit something!" Phoebe yelled.

"Leave a pole there and keep going," Brian called. "It could just be a rock." We kept moving up the slope while one of the rescue team members dug near Phoebe's pole.

Just a few steps later, I felt my pole hit something. "I found something!" I shouted. A woman in an orange jacket swooped down with a shovel. She slammed her shovel into the snow over and over, until I heard it hit something. Brian dashed over and started to dig, too. "There he is!" he yelled.

We all gathered around as they freed the man's face and arms. He was curled up, with his hands in front of his face. A paramedic ran over and checked to see if he was breathing.

"I think he'll be okay," the paramedic said. "He made a breathing space with his hands. That gave him just enough air."

Brian let out a big sigh. Then he smiled. From the moment he got the emergency call, Brian had been nothing but business, completely focused on the rescue mission. But now he grinned and lifted me in the air to give me a big bear hug.

"We found him, Carlos!" he said. Then he hugged the Friz, too. "Valerie, am I glad you picked this week to show up with your Magic School Bus!"

He looked around and shook his head in amazement. "You did really well, all of you. I am so proud of you," he said. "You saved two lives today." He grinned again. "It feels good, doesn't it?"

CHAPTER 8

Back at the lodge, we sat around a crackling fire and talked about what had happened.

"What did those skiers do wrong?" Ms. Frizzle asked.

"They didn't bring beacons," D.A. said.

"Or probes," I added.

"Wait a minute," Phoebe said. "How can you carry a 12-foot pole while you're skiing?"

"Oh, you don't have to," said Ms. Frizzle. "You can bring special ski poles that attach together to make a probe."

"What about shovels?" Keesha asked.

"A shovel is one of a rescuer's best tools," Brian agreed. "You can dig a hole five times faster with a shovel than with your hands. That's important when every second could be the difference between life and death."

"And shouldn't they have brought a radio?" Tim said.

"Yes," Brian said. "Thank goodness they had a cell phone. But a radio would have allowed them to receive an avalanche warning and head back *before* they got in trouble. Anything else?"

"They shouldn't have crossed that slope together," Phoebe said.

"That's right. But at least James stayed behind. If he hadn't, no one would have even known they were missing." There was a silence as we all thought about that.

"They did do some things right, though," Brian said. "James stayed at the scene, instead of leaving for help. If he'd left, it would have been too late by the time he got back. And the man who was buried probably saved his life by getting his hands in front of his face. He cleared out just enough space to breathe."

"I think their biggest mistake was going out there at all," Arnold said.

"You're right, Arnold," Brian said seriously. "The best way to protect yourself from an avalanche is to stay out of its way. They were very, very lucky that we happened to be nearby. You should always check for avalanche warnings before hitting the slopes, and once you're out, keep an eye out for any warning signs, like cracks and drifts."

"Where do you learn about stuff like that?" I asked.

"If you really want to be a backcountry skier, the first thing you should do is take a training course from the Mountain Rescue Association or the National Ski Patrol."

"Do you teach training courses?" Wanda asked.

Brian nodded. "I've given talks all over Colorado, and other places, too."

"Wow!" I said. "You have the best job in the world."

"Oh, it's not my job, Carlos," Brian said with a smile. "I work here in the lodge. I just do rescue work in my spare time."

Everyone gaped at him.

"Brian is a volunteer," said Ms. Frizzle. "The whole Mountain Rescue Team is made up of volunteers."

"You know, like a volunteer fire department. Just neighbors who want to pitch in and help other people," Brian said.

"You mean . . . you do all this for free?" Tim asked. "Why?"

Brian laughed. "You were volunteers today, too. How did it make you feel when you saved those people?" he asked.

Tim thought a moment. "Happy. And proud," he said.

"Scared. And tired," Arnold said.

Everyone laughed. I knew what Arnold meant. But I also found myself standing up a little straighter, thinking about what we had done.

"I do it because I love it," Brian said. "Volunteering with the Mountain Rescue

Team is the most satisfying thing I've ever done."

"Ms. Frizzle?" I said. "When we get back to school, maybe we can find a volunteer project the whole class can do."

"That's a great idea, Carlos," the Friz said.

Brian ruffled my hair. "Once you start, you won't want to stop. My mother taught me about doing volunteer work when I was your age, and I've been doing it ever since."

"I can't wait to join a rescue team when I grow up," Phoebe said.

"Me, too," I agreed.

"Well, you've already done more than I ever did at your age," Brian said. "But then again, I didn't have a Magic School Bus!"

Questions to Ask Yourself
in Avalanche Country
by Carlos [Future Ski Patrol Leader]

1. What are the weather conditions? Have there been recent heavy snows? Has the wind or temperature changed drastically?

2. Have you noticed fractures in the snow? If you can see cracks, the snow might not be safe. If you have heard any cracking or "whumping" sounds, that might be a sign that snow is shifting.

3. Are you carrying a beacon and is the signal turned on?

4. Is there a safer way to get where you are going without crossing a possible avalanche path?

CHAPTER 9

The next day, we were back in school finishing up our winter weather projects. We'd gotten more hands-on experience than we had bargained for!

"Carlos, aren't you getting hot in that jacket?" Dorothy Ann asked.

I proudly glanced down at my orange rescue squad jacket. Brian had given it to me just before we left Colorado. No way was I going to take off that jacket!

"As a matter of fact, D.A.," I said, "I feel pretty cool in this coat!"

I went back to work on my avalanche rescue project.

Across the room, the other kids were gathered around Wanda's ice cube insulation project. She was testing different materials to see which one was best at keeping an ice cube from melting. Meanwhile, Dorothy Ann was studying more snowflakes.

"Ms. Frizzle," Arnold said, "isn't it about time for recess?" He pointed out to the playground. It was covered with more than six inches of newly fallen snow.

"Can you believe it?" I said. "The snow followed us all the way back from Colorado!"

"Actually, Carlos," Dorothy Ann corrected me, "it was a cold front from the north meeting a warm front from the south that brought the snow — with a little help from the jet stream."

The world would always have a scientific explanation with D.A. around.

Ms. Frizzle checked her special watch that had icicles for hands.

"Arnold, you're right," she said. "It's recess time, and I know why you want to get

outside. This snow is nice and sticky — great for making a snowman."

"Just like my project says," replied Arnold.

"Okay, 15 minutes for recess," Ms. Frizzle said. "I have to finish up some work in here first, but then I'll join you outside."

Wanda and Phoebe started to giggle, but Arnold gave them a look that made them stop.

We all pulled on our winter gear and headed for the door. Arnold picked up his backpack and took it along.

"Okay, let's hurry up," Arnold told the rest of us. "We only have 10 minutes to make the best snowwoman ever!"

I helped roll the big snowball that made the middle of the snowwoman. Three of us lifted it onto the even bigger ball Arnold had made that morning. Then Arnold, Dorothy Ann, and Tim put a smaller snowball for the head on top of the other two, and added eyes, a nose, and a mouth.

"Open your backpack, Arnold," D.A. said. "Hurry up. We don't have much time!"

Arnold unzipped his backpack and first pulled out an orange winter scarf with long fringe on the ends. He put it on top of the snowwoman's head and then added Ms. Frizzle's winter hat, which he had borrowed from her cubby. Dorothy Ann added some icicle earrings as a final touch.

We heard the door from the classroom

open behind us. We crowded in front of the snowwoman as Ms. Frizzle walked toward us.

"Surprise!" we yelled, and jumped aside.

Ms. Frizzle was surprised all right. Then she laughed and said, "See, Arnold? Didn't I say you'd get to make the best snowman ever? Hold still, everyone, and I'll take a picture for Arnold's report."

Join my class on all of our
Magic School Bus adventures!
Look for these exciting chapter books:

The Truth about Bats
The Search for the Missing Bones
The Wild Whale Watch
Space Explorers
Twister Trouble
The Giant Germ
The Great Shark Escape
The Penguin Puzzle
Dinosaur Detectives
Expedition Down Under
Insect Invaders
Amazing Magnetism
Polar Bear Patrol
Electric Storm